FROG

WENT A-COURTIN'

Retold by JOHN LANGSTAFF

With pictures by FEODOR ROJANKOVSKY

SCHOLASTIC INC.
New York Toronto London Auckland Sydney

For my Carol
who was the first to give me
the fun of singing with children

AWARDED THE CALDECOTT MEDAL AS

"The most distinguished American picture book for children"

IN THE YEAR OF ITS PUBLICATION

20 19 18   0 1 2/0

Printed in the U.S.A.   08

THE STORY OF THIS STORY

Nobody knows how or when this story really started. We do know that it was written down in Scotland more than 400 years ago. But it has always been the kind of story that was *told* and *sung* to children, instead of being *read* to them. The grandfathers and grandmothers sang it to the mothers and fathers, and the mothers and fathers sang it to their children, and finally it got to us. Sometimes the grownups might forget some of the words, and the children would make up words they liked better, and put them in the song. And so the ballad, or story, on down through all these hundreds of years, always changed a little bit as each new person tried to sing it. Everyone liked his way best.

When America was first discovered and the people came from England and Scotland to live here, they brought this ballad along with them, and they kept on singing it to the children. It spread all over the country with the people as they moved from the North and South to the West. The story of the "Frog and the Mouse" became a part of America, and belongs to all of us today.

For this book, I made one happy story out of the different ballads that are sung in many parts of America and other countries about the frog and the mouse and their little animal friends. So you see that hundreds of grownups and children have helped me to make this book for you to read, and I have just put together the stories they sang without changing a word of theirs.

The music is only one of many tunes for the ballad, but it is the easiest I know, and the children of the southern Appalachian mountains sing *their* story to it.

J. L.

Frog went a-courtin', he did ride,
Sword and pistol by his side.

When upon his high horse set,
His boots they shone as black as jet.

He rode right up to mouse's hall,
Where he most tenderly did call:

"Oh, Mistress Mouse, are you within?"

"Yes, kind frog, I sit to spin."

He took Miss Mousie on his knee,
"Pray, Miss Mouse, will you marry me?"

"Without my Uncle Rat's consent,
I would not marry the president!"

Then Uncle Rat he soon comes home.
"Who's been here since I've been gone?"

"A pretty little dandyman," says she,
"Who swears he wants to marry me."

"Where will the wedding breakfast be?"
"Way down yonder in a hollow tree."

"What will the wedding breakfast be?"
"Three green beans and a black-eyed pea."

"Who will make the wedding gown?"
"Old Miss Rat from Pumpkin Town."

Then Uncle Rat gave his consent,
And that's the way the marriage went.

The first to come in was a little white moth,
To spread on the tablecloth.

Next to come in was a big black bug,
On his back was a cider jug.

Next to come in was Mister Coon,
Waving about a silver spoon.

Next to come in was a spotted snake,
Passing 'round the wedding cake.

Next to come in was a bumblebee,
A banjo buckled on his knee.

Next to come in was a nimble flea,
To dance a jig for the bumblebee.

Next to come in was the old gray goose,
She picked up her fiddle and she cut loose!

Next to come in were two little ants,

Fixin' 'round to have a dance.

Next to come in was a little ol' fly,

He ate up all the wedding pie.

Next to come in was a little chick,

He ate so much it made him sick.

The last to come in was the old tom cat.
He says: "I'll put a stop to that!"

The frog and the mouse they went to France.
And this is the end of my romance.

Frog's bridle and saddle are laid on the shelf.
If you want anymore, you must sing it yourself!

Frog went a-court-in', he did ride, *h'm* _____ *h'm* _____

_____ Frog went a-court-in', he did ride,

sword and pis-tol by his side, *h'm* _____ *h'm* _____ .